SUCCESSORIES®

Motivational
Minutes

By
Don Essig

CAREER
PRESS

Franklin Lakes, NJ

MOTIVATIONAL MINUTES
ISBN 1-56414-290-6, $13.00
Cover design by The Hub Graphics Corp.
Printed in the U.S.A. by Book-mart Press

To order this title by mail, please include price as noted above, $2.50 handling per order, and $1.50 for each book ordered. Send to: Career Press, Inc., 3 Tice Road, P.O. Box 687, Franklin Lakes, NJ 07417. Or call toll-free 1-800-CAREER-1 (NJ and Canada: 201-848-0310) to order using VISA or MasterCard, or for further information on books from Career Press.

Library of Congress Cataloging-in-Publication Data
Essig, Don.
    [148 motivational minutes]
    Motivational minutes / by Don Essig.
        p.   cm. -- (Successories)
    Originally published: 148 motivational minutes. Lombard, Ill. :
Successories Pub., 1994.
    ISBN 1-56414-290-6 (hardcover)
    1. Motivation (Psychology)   I. Title. II. Series.
BF503.E87   1997
158.1--dc21   96-39983
                                                              CIP

3605993)

APR 17 1997   81

Contents

Introduction

Don Essig's Motivational Minutes have been designed to help people focus, think and act more positively in their personal and professional lives. Each Motivational Minute is written to help the reader focus more clearly on the positive aspects of successful living by identifying personal strengths and the influential others in one's life. Personal and professional goal-setting is a major component of Motivational Minutes as well.

Don recommends that after reading each of the Motivational Minutes you take a pencil and paper and answer in writing each of the following questions:

1. How can this Motivational Minute help me in my personal life?
2. How can this Motivational Minute help me in my professional life?

Doing this activity can help the reader gain a fuller understanding of the Motivational Minute and also help to design a more complete daily plan for life.

MAKING CHOICES

You've no doubt heard the saying "Today is the first day of the rest of your life." But have you ever really thought about what this means? We *can* make each new day a fresh opportunity, a chance for new choices and new goals. With the beginning of each new day you have the opportunity to start with a clean slate. So, from now on, when you wake up each morning, welcome the new day. Think about how you can get the most out of each minute. Set a game plan, and then live every moment of the day pursuing your own personal excellence. It's a choice you will never regret.

MANY ALTERNATIVES

Willa Foster, a philosopher, once said, "Quality is never an accident; it is always the result of high intention, sincere effort, intelligent direction, skillful execution, and it represents the wise choice of many alternatives." In everything we do, we always have alternatives to choose from. It is striving to make the right choices that continues to ensure quality in our personal strengths. Those who make a sincere effort to make themselves the best possible persons they can be have taken the first step in the pursuit of personal excellence.

LIFE'S ACCOMPLISHMENTS

Take a moment and think about what things you do best. At what have you been most successful in life? It's odd how many people will spend an unfair amount of time thinking about what mistakes they've made rather than their accomplishments. Take a few minutes and think about what you have accomplished within the last day. How about the last month...or year? Think about what you want to accomplish both short- and long-term. And then go after those goals. But when you do look back, be proud. When you really start looking around, you'll see that you've actually accomplished a lot!

SIGNIFICANT OTHERS

Most people think of Significant Others as spouses or mates. But what about all the other people who play a significant role in your life? Maybe a relative, your best friend, a teacher or a co-worker. Oftentimes they have helped us model our behavior or strengthened our values. So, why not take a minute today and call or write to some of the Significant Others in your life? Thank them for how they have helped shape your world. Let them know they're special. It will most certainly make their day—and just think of how good it'll make you feel.

MOTIVATIONAL MINUTE #4

TRADING MY LIFE

You may have heard the saying "What I do today is important because I'm trading a day of my life for it." But have you ever really thought about what it means? It's probably impossible to plan every 1,440 minutes of the day. But one thing you must plan for every day is time for yourself. Start setting a few minutes aside every day just for you. Maybe it's taking a walk or driving home from work. Use this time to think about your life and what you want from it. Enjoy yourself and make every day count because you're trading a day of your life for it.

LIFE SPACES

Surrounding you every day, whether it's at home or in your office, are your Life Spaces. You can do a lot to these spaces to make them more positive, comfortable and motivating. Maybe it's a coat of paint in a cheerful color, or surrounding yourself with photographs. Try hanging a positive quotation or poem that will inspire you daily. Someone once told me that you cannot do much about the length of your life, but you can do a whole lot about width and depth. So, think about improving your Life Spaces. I guarantee, it will make a world of difference.

UNDER THE HILL

You no doubt know some people who continually fret about their age. Maybe one of those persons is you. We often hear excuses about being too old, too burned out or unable to learn anymore. Too many people give up on their hopes and dreams when they reach *that age*. It's true that you can do anything if you put your mind to it—no matter what your age! So take a few minutes today to think how you can achieve your goals. Rebuild your enthusiasm for life because life is too precious and too short to not live it to the fullest.

MOTIVATIONAL MINUTE #7

BURDEN OR OPPORTUNITY

Have you ever fantasized about what it would be like if you had no burdens or problems in life? Many people do. Unfortunately, it will always remain a fantasy because nobody goes through life problem-free. The key is identifying your problems and then quickly following through on a plan of action to remedy the situation. When you are faced with a problem, take a minute to analyze how it came to be and think about how you can turn it into an opportunity. Formulate a game plan and you'll soon see no problem is insurmountable!

MOTIVATIONAL MINUTE #8

POSITIVE OVER NEGATIVE

Have you noticed how many people are so quick to criticize and complain? Does it often seem that some people dwell on the negative? Well, there is one way to overcome this problem. Don't practice negative talk yourself. Take the time to praise the people around you. Thank them for their contributions. Congratulate or compliment someone for a job well done. Send a thank-you note. Giving thanks and praise will make a difference. And you can bet it will come back to you in more positive ways than you can ever imagine.

MOTIVATIONAL MINUTE #9

ACCENT THE POSITIVE

Is there someone around you who always says "It'll never work"? That can create a current of negativity that is hard to overcome. If you start making an effort to surround yourself with positive people, you will find the attitudes of positive people to be very contagious. Take five minutes and make a list of the positive behaviors you have exhibited and then make a conscious effort to start thinking and behaving more positively. It's amazing what an impact it will have on your entire outlook and your well-being.

MOTIVATIONAL MINUTE #10

OPPORTUNITY

Does it ever feel like you're missing something in life? That maybe it's time to try something different? Maybe you're afraid of change—that's normal. However, it is amazing how many people don't believe they can do anything other than what they're doing now. Have you looked for new opportunities lately? Ann Landers once said, "Opportunities are usually disguised as hard work, so most people don't recognize them." Keep your eyes open! You'll be surprised at all the fresh opportunities that await you.

MOTIVATIONAL MINUTE #11

PLAN TO PLAN

You've spent a large part of your life planning your work, your career, your personal affairs and your travel. Have you ever stopped and thought about how much time you actually spend planning? Well, it's pretty amazing. Without this important time, life would be a hodgepodge of activities with no direction or purpose. Take time today to think about how you successfully plan—and what might happen if you don't! Every day, take time to plan. You'll see that it makes a world of difference.

CREATIVITY

Do you consider yourself a creative person? When people are asked if they are creative, most reply maybe or no. Just because you don't write music or draw pretty pictures doesn't mean you aren't. Every day you think up new ways of doing things, create conversations, write memos, plan meals, solve problems and so on. Those are all examples of creativity. Think about all the creative things you do every day! Now's your chance to think about all of the creative talent you have. You'll soon see that you have more creativity than ever!

A SIMPLE IDEA

Did you ever notice people who can take someone else's idea and put a long list of barriers in front of it? What seemed like such a simple, reasonable and workable plan, all of a sudden became a nightmare of hurdles! Many times the barriers become so great that the idea is set aside completely and never considered again. Do you have an idea that you have been contemplating? Try to see how simple you can make it, so it can be tried. Then test the idea in order to help it be successful. You'll discover how many ideas can and will work if given half a chance.

MOTIVATIONAL MINUTE #14

CHANGE IS GOOD

Have you ever thought about all the changes we make in life? We choose to change jobs, homes, offices, friends, furniture, clothes, cars, even hairstyles. Maybe you know people who are forever resistant to change. They may even make themselves ill by this drive to maintain sameness. Remember that change is an ongoing aspect of our lives and society. Bruce Barton, noted philosopher, once commented, "When you're through changing, you're through." Write down the changes you have made recently. Are you through changing or are you just beginning?

PLAN AHEAD

Have you ever found yourself with a long list of things to do and a frustrated feeling about where to start? Do you have a to-do list? Most people keep lists or reminder notes to plan their days. Some people even plan for a month at a time—but very few go further than that. Planning for one year and five years from now is in many ways more important than planning for just today. Take some time today to think about the next one to five years, and don't just think about it, write it down. It will give you direction, confidence, positive feelings and hope.

MOTIVATIONAL MINUTE #16

IT'S THE RULE!

Did you ever stop to think about all the rules and restrictions we face every day of our lives? We set rules at home, at work, in the car and even when we eat. Most of the rules are written and obvious! Those are the easy rules. The difficult rules are those we use to stifle our own creativity and pretend that we can't do things when we actually can. What is something you've always wanted to do, but your own *can't* rules keep you from trying it? Who can help you? What strengths can you apply? Make a new rule with yourself that you won't let the *I can'ts* stand in the way of your dreams.

IT'S NOT WASTED

You may have heard about all the money that corporations invest in time management seminars. These time management professionals come in and analyze how time is '"wasted." Well, sometimes thinking time is not wasted time. Does every to-do list have to have an organized format, or is it most important that we just get it written down? Take this time today and consider how you use your time most effectively. The most important thing is to get things done. It doesn't matter how you get there if it works for you.

INCREASING YOUR WEALTH

Have you noticed people around you who have capitalized on a strength or talent to make extra money? They're really no different from you except that they took an idea and ran with it. There are hundreds of success stories of people who have devoted their free time to inventions, writing, moonlighting and so on. Many of them have gained wealth they didn't expect. Have you assessed your strengths to see where you might be able to make extra money? Think about how you could make extra money by capitalizing on your strengths.

KINDNESS SPEAKS

Gene Bedley, national speaker on self-esteem, tells his audiences that "Kindness is the language the deaf can hear and the blind can see." In the midst of conflict and problem solving, being kind to one another will often lead to renewed creativity and motivation. It is possible to disagree and still work together. By simply being kind and listening to other people, a wide variety of ideas and proposals will come through. Use this time today to think about ways that simple kindness can have an even greater influence on your life.

LIFE'S TOO SHORT

In my program "Life's Too Short Not to Work Together," I try to get people to realize how much time is actually spent working alone, and how much of our lives is spent working and interacting with others. Think for a moment of all the things you do alone that don't affect anyone else. It should quickly become evident that everything we do impacts other people somewhere along the way. It is important to find ways to exchange words, feelings and signals that make for effective relationships. Take a minute today to think about how everything you do ultimately affects someone else.

MOTIVATIONAL MINUTE #21

ALL THINGS ARE POSSIBLE

Have you ever noticed how many seminars, television programs, classes and books there are on communication? People throughout the United States put a lot of emphasis on communication these days. Yet, we still lead the world in divorces, child abuse, and crime—all of which could be reduced through increased positive communication. I have a belief that communication begins with self-talk. Do you believe in yourself? Use your time today to make a list of all the things you have accomplished because you practiced positive self-talk communication.

MOTIVATIONAL MINUTE #22

BE A WINNER

Have you heard the saying "A winner listens, a loser just waits until it's his turn to talk"? It is so often true that listening is the most violated of communication skills. Many people hear the words, but don't get the message, simply because they are just waiting for their turn to talk. Listening takes concentration and an interest in what the other person is saying. How often do you catch yourself waiting until it's your turn to talk? How can you improve your listening skills? Share your ideas with someone else who can help you become a better listener.

ENDORPHIN POWER

Have you ever thought about humor playing a vital role in your good health? Putting humor and laughter into our lives can make a tremendous difference in our overall health and well-being. Norman Cousins, the late editor of *Saturday Review Magazine,* proved through his research with endorphins and adrenaline that feeling good has a large influence on our physical being. Finding the humor in life and laughing turns on the endorphin flow. Are you getting your share of laughter? Begin planning today how you can get more laughter and feeling good into your life.

SUCCESSFUL QUITTERS

Mae West once said, "You're never too old to become younger!" It's really sad to see how many people make themselves old too soon. They do that by maintaining bad health habits such as smoking, drinking, drug abuse and not eating properly. What steps have you taken to ensure a longer, healthier physical life for you or those around you? Are there some ways you can get rid of bad habits? Make a plan of action. If it's others around you, let them know you care about their health—offer your support. This is one time that it's good to be a quitter.

LIVING LONGER

One of my close friends, George Iannacone, once told me "Old age is a hardship, but a greater hardship is not to see old age." It's sad to see so many people who've retired and then do nothing with their lives! Looking forward to life and involvement in positive activities can do wonders for you! A happy, healthy mind will tell your body to stay healthy because you have lots more to do in life. What are you planning to accomplish in your lifetime? Make plans now on how you want to live the rest of your life.

MOTIVATIONAL MINUTE #26

ASK SOMEBODY

Throughout your life there have no doubt been times you've identified things that could use improvement. Maybe you've tried to eliminate a bad habit or improve a skill. Do you ever wonder if any of these changes have made a difference in your life? Well, there is one simple way to find out for sure—ask someone. Let others know you've been working on making a change and that you want their honest evaluation. People will be impressed with your desire to do better, and you'll no doubt get some valuable feedback along the way!

MOTIVATIONAL MINUTE #27

JOBS WITHOUT PRESSURE

John Wooden, the longtime famous basketball coach, when asked about the pressure of being the UCLA basketball coach, replied, "Show me a job without any pressure, and I'll show you a job that's not a good job." If we believe what John Wooden said, then there probably aren't any jobs without pressure of some kind. But remember that no pressure at all will probably result in no productivity. Think about your job for a minute. Maybe the pressure you have is simply helping you get it done better!

LEARN FROM EXPERIENCE

Robert Sinclair, educator and speaker, shared this idea in a conference: "We really don't learn anything from our experience. We only learn from reflecting on our experience." Interesting idea, isn't it? Most of us have been told our entire lives that we learn from experience. What I think Sinclair really meant was that when we take some time to think and reflect, that's when the real learning takes place. So, why don't you take the time to think about what you've learned from reflecting on your experiences? I think you will find you've learned a lot!

COMPLIMENTS

Mary Kay Ash, in her famous book *Mary Kay on People Management,* wrote, "No matter how busy you are, you must take time to make the other person feel important." If people would take more time to think about the ways they can make others feel important, the reward would be quite simple—we would feel more important ourselves. Perhaps the best way is simply through the sharing of sincere compliments. Look today for ways to compliment those around you. It will make both you and the people around you feel important.

DATA FEEDBACK

In one of my seminars I try to emphasize and assist people in understanding the importance of what I call "data feedback." It is a system in which we collect information, verify whether or not it is true, do something with the information and evaluate our actions. Most importantly, it involves the old cliche "In case of doubt, check it out!" Too many people rush to make decisions without checking out the information. Have you found yourself in that situation recently? Take a minute today to think about how you check out information you receive before you act.

POSITIVE EMOTIONS

In his very popular book, *Anatomy of an Illness*, the late Norman Cousins stated that "Positive emotions are directly connected to positive chemical changes." Cousins proved this idea most convincingly as he healed himself from an incurable disease back in 1964. He found that a major contributor to healing was laughter—because of the flow of endorphins from the adrenaline system every time you laugh or feel good. With positive emotions, such as humor, you can also start the endorphin flow. Take a minute today and think about how you can get more positive emotions back into your daily life.

START SMALL

One of the participants in one of my programs anonymously sent me the following saying: "Think Big, Start Small!" The idea reminded me of why so many people often have difficulties with setting plans and goals. They set their goals high, but then try to reach all of them at once without working out a step-by-step process for achieving them. They get bogged down and overwhelmed by the task, and often quit. Take a minute today and think about how you can reach some goals you may not have reached by simply starting small—one idea and task at a time.

TRUST

Warren Bennis, educator and author, wrote recently that "Trust is the emotional glue that binds people together." What a great way to define this very important element in the lives of successful people. When we have high trust, things go along smoothly. When there is little or no trust, relationships tend to grind a lot. The sad fact is that many people have never been in a discussion of what trust really is. Take a minute today and make a list of all the qualities you think are part of trust. Then share them with someone you trust in your life.

SERVICE

My good friend and long-time mentor in education, Russel Tompkins, taught me that "Service is the rent we pay for our space on earth." For decades Russ donated his time and energy to the teaching of citizenship classes to immigrants, and helped them become patriotic citizens of our country. What service do you provide for your space? How many ways have you given of your time and energy to help others who may not be as fortunate as you? Take some time today and think about how you continue to pay for your space on earth with your ongoing service to others.

MOTIVATIONAL MINUTE #35

ADVERSITY

Someone once said that "Success isn't necessarily being the best. Success is handling the worst." How many people do you know who continually amaze you by how they handle life when it seems to be one setback after another for them? There are thousands of stories of people who have pulled themselves up from the depths of defeat by applying their strengths, setting new goals and using what they had. Think about some adversity you are dealing with at this time. List the strengths you have to work through it. You may find yourself out of the problem sooner than planned.

REWARDS AS TASKS

In his recent book, *Common Denominator of Success*, Albert Ian Gray wrote, "Successful people do things that failures don't like to do." How many people do you know who shy away from doing things simply because they don't like doing them? In every family and every job, there are tasks that someone won't like doing. Perhaps it's because we tend to focus too much on the task, instead of the reward received from doing the task. Successful people focus on the feeling of accomplishment. Think about the feeling of pride you recently had when you finished a project.

HARD WORK

Ann Landers, the very popular columnist, said, "Opportunities are usually disguised as hard work, so most people don't recognize them." Perhaps the problem is that the term "hard work" is a term that most people perceive as a negative one. So let's change the term to "smart work." Smart work is simply taking the strengths we have, combining them with the kindness of the people who help us in our lives, setting some plans and taking on the opportunity with enthusiasm. Then it is not perceived as hard work, but really intelligent effort which you have the strengths to do.

MOTIVATIONAL MINUTE #38

PITY PARTIES

Professional golfer and fun person, Lee Tre-vino, once told a reporter interviewing him, "No matter how bad you've got it, you only have to go a mile from your house to find someone who's got it a lot worse," Perhaps no truer words were ever spoken about why many people spend so much time in their lives in what I call pity parties. They don't take the time or make the effort to see what other people are experiencing. Take a minute today and think about some people who would probably think you have a lot. Maybe your situation won't seem so bad after all.

MOTIVATIONAL MINUTE #39

WINNERS

A smart coach once said, "Winners are just ordinary people making an extraordinary effort." Winners experience great success, they give the extra effort, they plan and they practice their plan, and they don't put down those around them who don't win as often. Most of them are just ordinary folks—like you and me—who use what they have to the maximum ability. So, how do they do it? Probably by taking lots of time to think out where they are going, and then using what they have to practice getting there.

UNDERESTIMATED TALENTS

In December of 1990, I had the privilege of hearing Alvin Law speak at a conference in Toronto. He said, "Never underestimate the talents and abilities of people." He shared his experiences as he demonstrated on his drums the talent he had used to win the Canadian National High School championship. Pretty amazing, huh? Well, not as amazing as when you watched and listened to him share all this with no arms. Alvin Law was born with no arms, and he was still able to use the strengths and talents he had to become successful. Are you using all your talents today?

LIFE CONTROL

Ashleigh Brilliant, the clever originator of over five thousand of his now famous "Pot Shots," wrote, "I would like to speak to whoever is in control of my life, and suggest some improvements." Well, who is in control of your life? Did you ever realize that except for the length of time we live, we really have control of most everything else? Take some time today and make a list of those potential improvements in your life, then match the list with all your skills and talents. Use your strengths to gain what you want.

MOTIVATIONAL MINUTE #42

SELF-TALK

Denis Waitley, motivational speaker and writer, says, "You are what you watch and think." Did you ever realize that your self-talk is your greatest communication skill? From your self-talk you can communicate to others hope, optimism, pride and positive attitude. How you talk to yourself and what you say inside controls all of what you eventually say on the outside. Do you talk positive to yourself, or are you always looking at mistakes you make and the fears you have? Take a minute today and analyze your self-talk. Only you can move it to the positive.

MOTIVATIONAL MINUTE #43

DIA PHORON

"Excellence" is a great word! It has been used in many forms throughout our country in recent years as a goal or a condition we would like to achieve. Many excellence awards have been given to schools, businesses and agencies. Ron Williams, a longtime postal worker, shared with me a little Greek phrase—*Dia Phoron*. It is the Greek phrase for excellence. The meaning is what excited me. It simply means "Follow through." Lots of people have great ideas and little follow-through. Do you want to reach excellence in your life? Then try a little *Dia Phoron*.

WHERE YOU WANT TO BE

Lawrence J. Peter, author and speaker, once told a group, "If you don't know where you are going, you will probably end up somewhere else." Do you know where you are going? Have you made a list of the things you want to do in life, places you want to go, or, more importantly, things you may want to be? If you haven't, you may end up someplace else. Making three lists can help you understand where you are going, and can also help you recognize those opportunities when they come along.

MOTIVATIONAL MINUTE #45

HUNCHES

Have you had any hunches lately? A participant in one of my seminars recently shared
with me that "A hunch is really creativity trying to tell you something." Those who pursue
their hunches are the ones who are maximiz-
ing their creativity. It may be an entirely new
idea to the world. That hunch might be your
next step toward personal excellence. But you
have to let it out, share it with people, collect
your information and try it out. If you don't,
you may be ignoring one of the most important ideas ever conceived. Don't underestimate your hunches. Take them out and test
them.

MOTIVATIONAL MINUTE #46

TRY NEW IDEAS

A smart teacher once reminded her class that "There are really no mistakes in life—there are only lessons." If we are going to continue to grow, then we must understand that growth is nothing more than a continuous process of trying new ideas, discarding the ones that don't work—sometimes known as failures— and keeping the ideas that do work. Unfortunately, many people shy away from trying new ideas because of the fear of failure. Innovative people are those who not only find the new ideas—they try them.

FLEXIBLE PEOPLE

If you had to pick a particular strength of successful people, which one would you pick? Well, a school custodian sent me this one to think about, saying that it hangs on the refrigerator door in his home as a reminder to all of his family. It goes like this: "Blessed are the flexible, for they shall not be bent out of shape." Did you ever notice how inflexible people can get out of shape, often whining or stretching their face at the suggestion of a new idea? Take a minute today and think about how flexible you are. Do you jump to conclusions? Flexible people think first!

MOTIVATIONAL MINUTE #48

UNLEARNING

In another Motivational Minute, I talk about the new and renewed learning that goes on in your life every day. Well, there is a third kind of learning—unlearning. So, what is it? Unlearning is the simple process of dumping the ideas you have learned previously that no longer fit. You really cover up the old memory cells with new ideas. Unlearning is moving forward in life, instead of rejecting new ideas. How many new ideas did you hear today? You can replace the old ones that may not fit anymore with new fresh ones. This is unlearning!

MOTIVATIONAL MINUTE #49

BIG PEOPLE

In one of the Dennis the Menace cartoons, Dennis is seen telling his friend Joey, "If it wasn't for Mr. Wilson, there'd be a big empty space in the world." That reference by Ketchum, the cartoonist, to the portly Mr. Wilson, reminds me that many of us have people in our lives who are very big people to us. We need to express to them often how big they actually are in our lives. Take a minute today and drop a note to some of those "big people" with a simple, but very sincere thanks for the part they play in your life.

YOUNG AS YOU THINK

Bob Hope, perhaps America's finest comedian, once said that "Excitement in what you're doing is the most important thing, and the next is to not think about your age all the time." How many people continually use the excuse of being too old for not doing new and exciting things in their lives? Grandma Moses painted 1,500 paintings after she was 80. George Burns was still acting and writing books in his mid-90s. Age is all an attitude. Think about your real age for a minute today. How young are you? How can you still get excited about what you are doing?

MOTIVATIONAL MINUTE #51

FIND ANSWERS

One of the most humorous but realistic state-ments I have heard about life is this one: "This life is a test. It's only a test. If it had been an actual life, you would have received further instructions on where to go or what to do." Are you one of those sitting around waiting for more instructions on what to do in your life? Or are you someone who is out finding the answers to the questions yourself? Those who are out finding answers are passing the test of life—which is simply that there are no easy answers. Think about how you are out testing your life for success.

MAKING CHOICES

One of the greatest doctors of all time, Albert Schweitzer, was once asked what he would share with the world about what he had learned if he was told he had but five minutes left in life. He said, "If you have something important to do, don't expect the people to roll the stones out of the way." No truer words were probably ever spoken about those people who have had important goals they wanted to accomplish. There is always someone who will create obstacles for us to overcome before we can succeed. Think about how you might work around some stone rolled in your way recently.

START IMMEDIATELY

William James, the great writer and philosopher, said, "To change one's life start immediately and do it flamboyantly—no exceptions!" What a challenge! That's exactly why I tell my audiences that part of goal setting is to tell everyone what you are doing! Why not let everyone else get excited with you about changing your life and moving on to bigger and better things? Are you changing your life quietly and privately, or with a bit of flair? Think about how you can add a bit of flamboyance to your life!

MOTIVATIONAL MINUTE #54

LUCK

Lucille Ball, the late comedienne, once said to some friends, "Luck? I don't know anything about luck. Luck to me is something else—hard work—and realizing what is opportunity and what isn't." Just look at all the people in the world who believe strongly that they don't have any luck when they sit around and do nothing to make life happen. They miss the opportunities that come along. Are you waiting for the goose to lay the golden egg for you? Think about how to make your own opportunities today.

MOTIVATIONAL MINUTE #55

RESIDENT NUT

One of the funniest speakers I ever heard, Zach Clements, told his audiences, "Every workplace in America needs a resident nut!" What he meant was that every workplace needs some people to help others laugh, help others see the humorous side of work, put up the motivation posters, hang the funny cartoons and bring the favorite snack food. Does your workplace have a resident nut? Remember, every time you laugh at work, the endorphins flow out of the adrenaline system. You can help it be a more fun place.

SELF-PRIDE

During her lifetime, Eleanor Roosevelt worked with all types of people from every aspect of American society. Perhaps one of her most profound statements was when she said, "No one can make you feel inferior without your consent." Too many people go around telling others that they are "only" this, or "just" that. They never seem satisfied with the way they are. If you're not happy with who or what you are, make some effort to change it. Be proud of who you are, instead of using words such as "only" and "just" to feel sorry for yourself.

LEARN THROUGH EXPOSURE

David Gardner, educator and author, said, "We learn simply by being exposed to living." There are, in fact, two kinds of learning going on in your life whether you know it or not—new learning and relearning are happening to you even if you try to resist them. Your brain, with its nearly 10 billion memory cells, is taking in new and renewed ideas all the time. Take today's minute and focus on all the new and different things you come in contact with today. How much are you actually learning without knowing it?

MOTIVATIONAL MINUTE #58

THINK POSITIVE

One of my best friends, Roger Crawford, tells his audiences, "I don't know if a positive attitude works every time, but a negative one does." That's a pretty strong statement, considering that Roger was born with three fingers, three toes on his right foot, and a left leg that required amputation when Roger was just five. Yet, with these handicaps he became a star tennis player in high school and college, and is living proof that a positive attitude does work in difficult situations.

GROWING OLD

In one of his many inspirational songs, John Denver sings, "To grow old is to change, to change is to be new, and to be new is to be young again." We all know that growing older brings with it a number of changes. Sadly, many people focus only on the physical changes of growing old, allowing themselves also to grow old mentally and emotionally. Changes in our lives bring new ideas, exciting challenges and added hope to life itself. Take a minute today and think about how you are letting the changes in your life allow you to feel young again.

MOTIVATIONAL MINUTE #60

OLD LADY, YOUNG LADY

In the now famous picture drawn by a University of Oregon professor back in 1931—of the lady who looks young if you look at her one way, and old if you look at her another way—I'm reminded that each of us is really two people. It just depends on how we look at each other. In reality, all of life is simply a perception of what we see, and we interpret it the way we see it. So, think about how you look at life. Do you only look at the one side, or do you make an attempt to look at both sides?

INWARD SUCCESS

A friend of mine and an outstanding teacher in New York, Frank Meyer, reminded me one day, "When you bombard yourself with inward success, you don't have time to be negative." Frank Meyer constantly reminds himself of his successes. At age 16, while running cross-country he tripped, fell and detached the retinas of his eyes—not ever seeing anything again. Yet he took his strengths and became a teacher, letting go of the fact that he had no sight. Take a minute today and bombard yourself with inward success. You really won't have any time left to be negative.

GROWING

Ronald Osborn once shared with his audience, "Unless you try to do something beyond what you have already mastered, you will never grow." Successful people are always reaching beyond what they have already mastered. They are setting new goals, looking up and out instead of at the ground, and constantly seeking self-improvement and ways they can help others to improve. Take a minute today and think about those things you are reaching for. Have you updated your list of goals, or have you temporarily stopped growing?

PEOPLE WHO SURROUND US

The great teacher and writer of many books on the subject of love, Leo Bascaglia, reminds us that "We're made, mostly, by the people who surround us." We are continually influenced by those around us—family, friends, co-workers, neighbors. And we allow those influential others to help us learn and grow into our maximum potential selves. Think about all the talents and strengths you have as a result of the people who surround you. Take a minute today and think about how you might give those same strengths and talents to someone else.

MISSED OPPORTUNITY

I have mentioned in other Motivational Minutes the large number of people who dwell on the negative, creating lifelong pity parties for themselves because of some failures they have experienced. Well, Henry Ford said, "Failure is the opportunity to begin again, more intelligently." If we analyze in detail why we experienced those failures, and what caused them, we will certainly be more intelligent. Are you dwelling on failure right now? Take another look at it, and see what you may have missed that can turn it into a new opportunity.

THE BEST PRIZE

Many years ago, President Theodore Roosevelt said that "Far and away the best prize that life offers is the chance to work hard at work worth doing." To me, work worth doing is work where I can improve my own strengths and skills, and help others at the same time. Is the work in life that you are doing right now worth doing, or are you just biding your time? Take a minute today and think about your work, whether it is paid or volunteer, and see if it is helping you and others improve. If not, maybe it's time to look for a new prize.

MOTIVATIONAL MINUTE #66

HAVING DEMOCRACY

The late news genius, Walter Winchell, once told his listening audience that "Too many people expect wonders from democracy, when the most wonderful thing of all is just having it." In 1989, my wife Janet and I had the privilege of working and traveling in Eastern Europe before the Berlin Wall came down. It was a real eye-opening experience to see how people lived without democracy. We take so much for granted, when what we really have is unlimited opportunity in this democracy. Think today about how fortunate you are to have democracy.

MOTIVATIONAL MINUTE #67

SHORTEST DISTANCE

Recently I heard the master of music and humor, Victor Borge, tell his television audience, "Laughter is the shortest distance between two people." Have you noticed lately how close you are to those people you laugh with the most? They make us feel great, they help our outlook on life, they keep those positive endorphins flowing from the adrenaline system—but mostly, they're just fun to be with. Take a minute today and think about those who help you to laugh every day. They're probably some of your closest people also!

THE BEST THINGS

One of my favorite workshop presenters in Colorado, Shirley Henry-Lowe, told me on a recent trip to her state that "The best things in life are not things." I have talked many times in the Motivational Minutes about the people in our lives, but have you thought much about how important our pets are also? Have you heard about the hospitals in the country with their pet centers? Pets are allowed to come and visit also, because they help our endorphins flow and speed up healing. If you have a pet, take a minute today and think how good it makes you feel.

FLOWERS ARE RED

In his "Flowers Are Red" song, the late singer Harry Chapin sang about the little boy who was conditioned into painting all his flowers red and his leaves green. Have you also been conditioned into doing everything the same way all the time? Did someone in your past do a good job of stifling your creativity and getting you in line? Well, it's time to paint the flowers another color. Think about the ways you can get out of the same corner or rut you are painted into. Take advantage today of your own personal creativity and go for it!

95 PERCENT WORKS

One of the facts I discovered in my working with groups is that about 95 percent of everything that people do every day works! And on many days, 100 percent of what they do works! Still people tend to spend a lot of time focusing on the five percent that didn't work, and they miss the satisfaction of feeling the many successes they have. A really sad fact is that too many people don't take the time to really think about everything they do every day that actually works. What did you do yesterday that worked? Make a list. You should be pleasantly surprised.

MOTIVATIONAL MINUTE #71

CONTROL CENTER

One of the constant reminders that Norman Cousins gave to his medical students at UCLA was this: "The control center of your life is your attitude." Negative attitudes lead to illness, feelings of defeat and downhill thinking. Positive attitudes lead to hope, love, caring, fun and endorphin flow from the adrenaline system. And you control all of it with your attitude. Take a few minutes today and think about how a little attitude adjustment for you might start those endorphins flowing again! It'll feel great!

PROBLEM

Have you ever noticed how many people use the word "problem"? And how many times it gets said every day? The really sad fact is that often when the word is said, we discover afterwards that there wasn't any problem after all. I tell folks in my workshops that many times if you say the word "problem" you will have one, whether you really have one or not. So, call it something else. I don't care what, but not every situation that gets labeled a "problem" is one. Keep track today of how many times you hear the word used and how many times there really isn't any problem after all.

DO IT WELL

One of my mentors, teacher and friend, Phil Runkel, said at his retirement celebration, "People who don't like what they're doing don't do it very well." Phil's comment helped me to discover that I didn't like what I was doing at age 46, and helped me to make a major career change in my life. Do you really like what you are doing? If you don't, chances are you aren't doing it very well. Take some time today and make a list of the things you would really like to do. Make your plan and go for it.

100 PERCENT OF THE SHOTS

Roger Crawford, my good friend, motivational speaker and tennis player—although he has only three fingers and an amputated leg—tells people, "You miss 100 percent of the shots you don't take." Not even the greatest athletes in the world, regardless of their sport, ever hit 100 percent of the shots they take. But they still keep taking them, even when they know they can't be perfect. Are you missing some shots in life simply because you aren't taking them? Get those goals written down today, and start taking some shots you haven't been taking.

UNDER CONSTRUCTION

The late marketing and promotions entrepreneur, Gary McNaught, once said, "The road called excellence is always under construction." Too many people believe that if they just put up the banners and wave the excellence flags, they will have it. Unfortunately, it doesn't work that way. People have to realize that to reach excellence they sometimes have to fill in the potholes, be flexible in their plans and be ready to adjust when obstacles come along they weren't planning on. Don't think about giving up on reaching excellence. Just be ready to make some adjustments, if needed, in order to finally get there.

MOTIVATIONAL MINUTE #76

THE ANSWER'S NO

I once saw a small poster hanging on a refrigerator in a friend's home that said, "If you don't ask, the answer's no!" That started me thinking about how many times in my own life I didn't ask the question for fear of being turned down in the answer. Or didn't ask the question for fear of looking stupid. Unfortunately, I will never know some of those answers. Maybe some would have been yes answers, but since I didn't ask, the answer remains no. Think about the questions you are hesitating to ask for fear of the no answer. You might as well ask, or the answer will be no.

MOTIVATIONAL MINUTE #77

NOT TOO OLD

Former major league baseball catcher Carlton Fisk, in a recent article, said, "The commitment to being the best you can be doesn't have an easy way out." He firmed up that belief more than 10 years ago, after he was traded for being labeled "too old" to be of any use to his team any longer. With commitment and dedication to working and thinking positive, Carlton Fisk remained a key player for the Chicago White Sox well into his 40s. Do you have commitment to being the best you can be? Think today about how you have to dedicate yourself and commit to making it work for you.

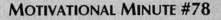

MOTIVATIONAL MINUTE #78

BELIEVE IN YOURSELF

One of the significant others in our family, Kim Pankey, mailed to me a briefcase bag tag that said, "Believe in yourself, and all things are possible." It's getting pretty worn out after five years of being hooked to my briefcase—mostly from people looking at it wherever I go. It is possible to do many things if you believe in yourself. But in order to, it is necessary to know who yourself is. Take a minute today and update your strengths list. Do you really know who you are? If you do, then you too can believe.

OPEN MIND

An anonymous participant in one of my early workshops sent me the statement, "An open mind affords the opportunity of dropping a worthwhile thought into it." It should be pretty obvious that people with closed minds are not receptive to a worthwhile thought being dropped in. If their minds are already made up in advance, there will be no opportunity to help them think about change and innovation. Take a minute today to think about how open-minded you are. Are you willing to consider new ideas, or is your mind already made up? You may be missing some great opportunities.

EMOTIONAL GLUE

In an earlier Motivational Minute, I shared the Warren Bennis quote, "Trust is the emotional glue that binds followers and leaders together." Trust also binds families together, neighborhoods together and good friends together. Groups that have high trust levels among the members move smoothly along. Those with low trust, grind. More than 95 percent of all the people in my audiences have never been in a meeting where trust was the agenda. Think about trust today, and how you might help others in your groups practice it more often.

SAY SOMETHING POSITIVE

George Smith, communications consultant, said to one of his audiences, "Say something positive to everyone you meet." Can you imagine what it would be like if everyone practiced that idea? Positive attitudes are only developed within people who practice thinking, acting and talking positive. The more we practice it, the more opportunities there are for people to switch from negative to positive. Take today and share something positive with everyone you meet. Then watch to see if it makes a positive difference for them.

MOTIVATIONAL MINUTE #82

SAY "HELLO"

I once read that a little smile adds a great deal to your face value. Have you noticed recently how many people smile when they look at you, or say "hello"? It's amazing how different I feel when I see someone who smiles rather than someone who doesn't smile, or worse, continually looks down at the ground. Do you smile a lot at others? How does it make you feel? I'll bet that almost every time you smile, you get one in return. Add some real face value to your looks today—smile at everyone you meet!

I'M AN OPTIMIST

The British leader Winston Churchill, during some of the toughest times of World War II, said, "I am an optimist. It does not seem too much use being anything else." Those with an optimistic attitude are those who have some goals, who look for the good in themselves and others and who are learning from the present but looking to the future. It's a funny thing, but the more I'm around optimistic people, the more optimistic I get. Think about how optimistic you are today. Optimism can surely help us out of those pity parties in life.

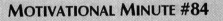

MOTIVATIONAL MINUTE #84

FAKE IT!

During one of my programs a few years ago, a gentleman came up to me at break time and asked, "What do you do when you don't have any enthusiasm?" So I gave him my answer, and in a not so quiet voice, I said—"Fake it!" Everyone has his or her own answer as to how you get enthusiasm. I happen to believe that if you fake it for 50 times or more, it then becomes you! Think about how you can fake some positive strengths you'd like to have. After a while you'll probably not have to fake it anymore. That will just be you!

SELL YOURSELF!

A retired salesman, when speaking to a group of trainees for his former company, said, "You don't sell products or services, you sell yourself." Did you know that was true for all of us, whether or not we are in the sales business or profession? Everyone we meet, every situation we are involved in with others all of our lives, is simply selling ourselves to others. Take a minute today and think about what you are selling to others. Do you like what you're selling? If not, the nice thing is that we can always make it better.

IMPROVEMENT COUNTS

In the previous Minute, I talked about not selling products or services, but selling yourself. It reminded me of a statement sent to me by an anonymous donor that said, "Improvement counts, no matter how small." If you are really selling yourself but you don't feel good about what you are selling, just remember to begin with one improvement at a time. Small as it may seem, it will count. After a while, you will have accumulated a large collection of improvements. Take a minute today and think about one small improvement you can make.

UPHILL THOUGHTS

I've talked before about the most important communication skill of all—your self-talk. I recently saw a quote that said, "You can't climb uphill by thinking downhill thoughts." If you are constantly putting yourself down or thinking about the bad things in life, you certainly will be keeping yourself from climbing uphill. Take a minute today and think about how you can change your inside communications by thinking positive, uphill thoughts. Remember, you are the only one who can hear them, so talk what you want to hear.

MOTIVATIONAL MINUTE #88

KIND

There is a wonderful little four-letter word that we don't hear very often—that word is "kind." Someone once said, "Be kind...everyone you meet has worries." Today would be a good day to start using the word "kind" if you haven't used it recently. Have you noticed how many people are actually kind to you? Think about how you can be kind to someone who probably has more worries than you. Maybe together we can get this important little word back into circulation.

MOTIVATIONAL MINUTE #89

CHANGE YOUR LIFE

An obviously wise person once stated, "To change your attitude is to change your life." That statement is perhaps the foundation of all the Motivational Minutes—helping people to begin thinking more seriously about how they can change their lives by changing their attitudes. And if you start by thinking a little change each day, eventually you can have major changes. How is your attitude? Take some time today and think about how you can be more positive. It'll change your life!

TRUE FRIENDS

A very smart person once said, "True friends don't sympathize with your weaknesses, they help bring out your strengths." Do you have some friends who need to have their strengths pointed out to them right now? Things may be so difficult for them, they have forgotten their strengths. You can help remind them of those strengths today. What a great opportunity for you to be a true friend. Help some of your friends who need a bit of help to look at their strengths. You may not notice right away, but you'll be looking at your strengths too.

TOO LITTLE

Albert Schweitzer, the marvelous teacher, musician and doctor, once reminded his co-workers, "He who begins too much accomplishes too little." In other words, if you have too many projects and ideas going it is very difficult to complete any of them totally. Taking one or two things at a time and seeing them to completion gives one the true feeling of accomplishment and satisfaction. Think about one thing you have going today that you could complete and have that very feeling.

MAKE YOUR DAYS COUNT

I once saw a sign hanging in a company office that read "Don't merely count your days—make your days count." Just look at all the folks who count their days to vacation, to retirement, to Saturday. And in the meantime, they may not be counting for very much in the process. Time goes on anyhow, so we don't need to spend much time counting. What we need to be counting is what we have gained or accomplished with the time we were given. Think about your recent accomplishments. You have probably counted for a lot!

MAKE A LIVING

"We make a living by what we get, but make a life by what we give." When I read those words from Winston Churchill, I was reminded of the words of my grandfather. He told me, "Give first, and you won't have to spend any time worrying about what you will get." So many people worry about getting that they forget to give back some of the strengths, talents and qualities they have been given. Take a minute today and think about something of yours that you might give to someone who needs it more than you.

OLDER THAN I AM

Bernard Baruch, the famous financier and statesman who lived to be a young 95, once said, "Old age is always 15 years older than I am." That philosophy about age is probably why he maintained his energy, creativity and positive enthusiasm for life right until the end. Too many people give up too early because they perceive themselves to be too old to change. What would happen to your life if you started thinking about old age being 15 years older than you? Crank up the energy and enthusiasm and go for it!

QUIT WORRYING

How about having a little fun today? Take a few minutes and make a list of the five things you are worrying about right now. Probably most of the things you write down you don't have control over at all. Marlene Williams, in her book *Survival Skills for Managers*, says, "Quit worrying over the things over which you have no control." That doesn't mean you'll stop worrying. But if you concentrate on things over which you *do* have control, you'll probably find yourself getting more things done. And you'll feel better not worrying about that other stuff!

LITTLE THINGS

In a company training room I once saw a very tiny poster on the wall near the floor. It said, "Learn to enjoy the little things—there are so many of them." Take today and look around you at all the little things you may be forgetting to enjoy: the pictures in your home or office, the office background music, the flowers, the wind in your face, your pet, your breakfast, your pillow. There are just so many little things that add up to make our lives. Think about them today, and notice how your life becomes larger.

LOTS OF LAUGHTER

One of the reasons why I enjoy listening to my good friends Jerry Allen and Mike Guldager on their radio show is that they fill the air with positive thoughts and lots of laughter. They work hard at sharing positive news and ideas with their listeners. And when we hear positive ideas, laughter and fun topics on a regular basis, it is so much easier to focus our thoughts and behaviors on the positive side. Take some time today and share some positive ideas with some folks you know—and laugh a little with them!

MOTIVATIONAL MINUTE #98

SELF-ESTEEM

One of my close friends and one of the origi-
nators of the self-esteem movement in the
United States, Robert Reasoner, told me "Self-
esteem is simple. You either feel good about
yourself, or you don't." Well, surrounding
yourself with the things and people that make
you feel good is the easy way to keep your
self-esteem at a high, positive level. Feeling
good doesn't cost much either—just feel it!
You are in control. Take some time today and
think about your self-esteem and then move it
up!

MOTIVATIONAL MINUTE #99

TRIUMPH

It's always fascinating to me how some people can take words and dissect them into a total message. For example, I recently saw the word "triumph" written with this phrase behind it—"Umph added to try." Triumph is already a powerful word, but that little phrase made it even more meaningful. In life, if we just put a bit of effort into something we didn't think we could do, we triumph! Have you put a bit of umph into a new idea lately? Today might be a great day for you to experience your own triumph!

> ### MOTIVATIONAL MINUTE #100

PERFECT LIFE

Did you ever notice how many folks are frustrated because they are looking for the perfect life? I heard someone say, "Like life, few gardens have only flowers." Each of us is going to find a few weeds and bugs among the flowers in our own lives. But they serve a worthwhile purpose. We have to keep working at removing them so we can enjoy the positive things in life. Take a look today at the positive parts of your life. Don't let the weeds overpower the flowers that exist for you.

> ### MOTIVATIONAL MINUTE #101

WELLNESS

The wellness movement in our country has been big for a number of years now. Someone once asked me my definition of wellness, and after thinking about it for a few days I decided that "Wellness is from the neck up, while fitness is from the neck down." Too many people spend too much time on their physical fitness programs, but still walk around with a negative attitude. In order to obtain wellness you have to challenge your own mind—stretch and exercise it like any other part of the body. Try some mind stretching today!

ICE CREAM

I just can't believe how many people let the stresses of life drag them down to the lowest level. Someone once told me that "Stress is like an ice cream cone—you have to learn to lick it." Licking stress only comes from using your talents and strengths to plan, set life goals, focus on the positive and surround yourself with positive people. Stress reduction never comes during a pity party. Take today and focus on the ways you can lick your stress. It'll feel just like eating your favorite ice cream cone!

GROW UP

I've talked a number of times about the positive aspects of laughter. During her magnificent acting career, Ethel Barrymore once remarked, "You grow up the day you have the first real laugh at yourself." Not only is laughter good for the endorphin flow into the body, but laughing at yourself shows everyone that you are human and capable of making mistakes just like anyone else. Have you done something funny recently? Don't forget to laugh at yourself for it.

TRY UPLOOK!

A close friend shared a little phrase with me that she saw pasted to the ceiling in an office that said, "When the outlook is poor, try up-look." You won't find the word "uplook" in the dictionary, but it certainly can be used to encourage the thinking of those with negative attitudes. To me, the word "uplook" indicates setting life goals and going for the top. How's your uplook today? Take a minute and see how looking up in life might help your attitude. Besides that, it's a fun word to share with someone.

MOTIVATIONAL MINUTE #105

JOB WELL DONE

The great American statesman and inventor, Benjamin Franklin, was once heard saying, "Well done is better than well said." How many people do you know who talk a good game, but when it comes time to doing the task, they are nowhere to be found? The really successful person is the one who talks from the experience of doing. Are you a person who *talks* well or *does* well? Think about the tasks you might do better. The respect for your ideas will be much greater if you actually did them.

GOLF AND LIFE

Once I ran across the following statement: "In golf and in life, it's the follow-through that makes the difference." It's not only a true statement in golf, however, it really is true in real-life situations. Whether or not we follow through on our ideas, our goals or our intentions, is what *really* makes the difference. If we don't follow through on our ideas, they become only wishes, and wishes by themselves don't do anything. Are you thinking about something today that requires more follow-through? You'll only know the difference if you go for it!

IT REALLY MATTERS

Katherine Graham, the noted publisher, once said to her audience, "To love what you do and feel that it matters—how could anything be more *fun?*" Are you having fun at what you are doing in life? Those who have fun at their jobs have a deep commitment to the fact that the results will make a difference for someone else. The negative parts of a job will get solved if people having fun at work go forward and solve the problems, not just let them hang on. Go forward today and have some fun—that's what *really* matters.

PLEASURE IN LIFE

Have you ever been told by someone else that you can't do something? Or, "It'll never work, so don't even try"? For some people, that can be really defeating. Someone once told me that "A great pleasure in life is doing what people say you can't do." And *what* a pleasure—to prove to others that you actually could do it! Accept the challenge, go out and learn the skills, set your mind to it and succeed. Have you been told lately that you can't do something? Think about the pleasure you can have by doing it anyway.

THINK AND DO

One of the world's great thinkers, John Charles Salak, shared this thought: "Failures are divided into two classes—those who thought and never did, and those who did and never thought." Well, I don't necessarily agree that those are the only two classes. I really believe that if you can get people to increase their thinking level about the things that really count in life, there would be a third class—those who thought and then went out and did. By increasing your thinking level, you can certainly increase your doing level!

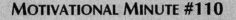

MOTIVATIONAL MINUTE #110

A DARING ADVENTURE

In spite of all her physical disabilities, Helen Keller did say that "Life is either a daring adventure, or nothing." How many people have made almost nothing out of their lives because they refused to dare themselves into new adventures? People like Helen Keller have provided role models for many who have chosen to take life head on! Are *you* considering a new adventure right now? Dare yourself to take it! If you don't, it could turn into nothing.

BEING YOURSELF

One of my friends reminded me recently that even though Thomas Edison was almost deaf, he didn't waste valuable time in his life trying to teach himself to hear. Instead, he concentrated on what he did best—thinking, creating and organizing. You have to begin by concentrating on what you do best. You have to be yourself, and let the strengths you have carry you through your goals and dreams. Spend some time today thinking again about your strengths and how they can lead you to a greater life.

IT'S NOT IMPOSSIBLE

In a workshop I attended recently, the presenter referred to a statement made long ago: "Every great achievement was once impossible." If something has never been done before, I suppose it would be easy to say it's impossible. However, if we've never tried it before, how will we really know? Are you considering an idea right now that you think might be impossible? How about giving it a try anyway? You never know—it might turn into a great achievement.

MOTIVATIONAL MINUTE #113

OAK TREE CLIMBING

Henry Ford once told a group of his employees, "Doers get to the top of the oak tree by climbing it. Dreamers sit on an acorn." I don't think there's anything wrong with dreaming, but for dreams to come true there has to be some effort on the part of the person doing the dreaming. Waiting for an unknown inheritance or hitting the right numbers in the lottery doesn't take much effort. Today might be the day to start climbing your own oak tree. At least you can be proud of the effort.

MOTIVATIONAL MINUTE #114

YOUR OWN FRONTIER

One of my favorite words has always been "frontier." And I guess I became even more enthused about the word when I heard this statement by Charles Kettering, the famous industrialist: "Where there is an open mind, there will always be a frontier." Most people think of frontiers as wagon trains or space ships, when in fact every new idea we hear, every new person we meet, or every new thought we ponder could be a new frontier. All of life is a new frontier, if we just explore it in new ways. Look for new frontiers today!

ONE GOOD COMPLIMENT

Mark Twain, perhaps one of America's most creative writers, once said, "I can live for two months on one good compliment." Well, I'm not sure that I can make it for two months, but a good compliment sure goes a long way to helping me have a positive day. How many good compliments have you given or received lately? Take some time today to call some people and give them a compliment. It will make you feel good—and they might make it for two months on the compliments you gave.

LIGHTEN THE BURDEN

Did you know that "No one is useless in the world who lightens the burden of it for anyone else"? One of England's greatest writers, Charles Dickens, made that statement many years ago. Dickens certainly lightened the load of many of his readers with his gifted writings. Are you helping others lighten their loads in life? Getting the chance to help others lighten their loads can help you go a long way on the road to enjoying a more positive life. Find someone today who needs your help to lighten a load.

FRIENDS WALK IN

I lost a close friend, Ellen Lind, to cancer. When I visited her two days before she died, she told me she was glad that I had the courage to come and visit her. All I could really think to say was a little saying I recalled from Walter Winchell, the great journalist, "A friend is one who walks in when others walk out." The real friends show up even if there isn't much they can do. Just being there is the test of the real friendship. Are there some folks out there today who need you to walk into their lives? Be a real friend.

WHAT YOU ARE

On a recent consulting trip to New York State, I was given the following statement by Jeff Gregory's parents, written by Jeff: "Though you are judged by the company you keep, you become only what you are." Jeff had tremendous potential to become a great writer. Unfortunately, he lost his life at age 17 in a tragic accident. He did leave this legacy, however, as one reminder that we need to focus on our strengths, on our potential and on our goals for life. Thank you, Jeff, for that reminder.

MOTIVATIONAL MINUTE #119

ORNAMENTS OF A HOUSE

During the holiday season, I'm reminded of a statement by Ralph Waldo Emerson, who once said that "The ornaments of a house are the friends who frequent it." Each of us is actually decorated with strengths and skills we have gotten from our many friends. We are the combination of the gifts they have given us, and the skills they have helped us obtain in life. This special time of year is a good time to reflect and think about how our friends have decorated our lives. Don't forget to let them also decorate your house during the holidays.

MOTIVATIONAL MINUTE #120

EFFORTS AND COURAGE

There is an important need to have written goals for our lives. President John F. Kennedy told us, "Efforts and courage are not enough without purpose and direction." It seems that many people are giving the effort and trying different things in their lives, but don't seem to be going anywhere. Perhaps it's because they forgot the most critical step—writing down the purposes for why they are doing those things! Take some time today and review and write your purpose in life. What are you trying to accomplish?

SIGHT WITHOUT VISION

Did you know that "The most pathetic person in the world is someone who has sight, but has no vision?" Those visionary words were shared by Helen Keller, who never saw anything during her entire life. Yet she had visions for herself and her life that carried her much further than some others who never see them. Being a visionary person simply means asking yourself the "why" questions about life. Why am I here? Why am I doing what I am doing? Why am I going in the direction I am going? Create your vision today. Ask yourself why!

FEED THE DESIRES

What are your personal desires, wishes and dreams? What have you been doing about reaching any of those thoughts? It is surprising how a desire will die if it is never fed. That feeding includes defining exactly what it is you wish, and creating a plan of action for getting at it. And write down the plan. Wishes and dreams not written down are only that— wishes and dreams. If you write them down they become meaningful goals that you can more easily picture and work on. Start today! Write down those dreams and feed those desires!

HUSTLING AND LUCK

Sam Levenson was one of my all-time favorite humorists and teachers, and he once bragged, "The more I hustled, the luckier I seemed to get." I've said that before to people—if you set those goals, make some lists and then start telling everyone what you are after, you'll be surprised at how many folks will help you find them. And that's called luck! The old cliche about making our own luck works! Don't let those crazy ideas go unshared. You never know when someone won't think they're crazy at all, help you find them, and you'll be the luckiest person today!

KEEP HOPE ALIVE

John Gardner, a most noted author and teacher, said, "A prime function of a good leader is to keep hope alive." Do you have any family, friends or acquaintances who are having trouble keeping up their hope right now? Well, it's your chance to be a leader! Maybe they need to have some help rethinking their lives, looking at their strengths and refocusing their goals. And you can be the leader. Usually, they just need to have a different viewpoint given to them, and you can show them the positive side of their lives today. You can keep hope alive.

LOVE IS THE MEDICINE

Dr. Karl Menninger, the famous psychiatrist, not only said it but practiced it daily in his Kansas clinic—"Love is the medicine for the sickness of mankind." Loving and caring was the foundation of the Menninger Clinic. He helped people to give and accept love into their lives as the way of countering the many negative aspects of life around them. All the other strengths we have and use really need loving and caring to surround them. Using love as the medicine, we have greater potential of helping those with attitude sickness.

MOTIVATIONAL MINUTE #126

CONCEIVE AND BELIEVE

Much too often we forget just how powerful the three-and-a-half pound mass between our ears really is. Those nearly 10 billion memory cells were put there for a purpose—to be used. David Sarnoff, the genius television magnate, said, "What the human mind can conceive and believe, it can accomplish." Do a little review today of what you have already accomplished in life. All of those accomplishments started with an idea, conceived in the mind, then believed and then completed. What's your latest idea? Well, believe it!

MIND IS A CLOCK

"The mind is like a clock that is constantly running down and must be wound up daily with good thoughts." This comment, by Bishop Fulton Sheen, has been the motivator for me to pursue the Motivational Minutes. We're surrounded every day by the potential of negative activities, ideas and thoughts. So we need to remind ourselves of the positive things that go on all the time, the things we sometimes forget. It's easy to get engulfed in the negative stuff. Take some time today and wind up your mind with all the positive things going on in your life.

MOTIVATIONAL MINUTE #128

ME BEST

Probably without being conceited or trying to be funny, an anonymous person once said, "Of all my relatives, I like me best." It's pretty funny when you first think about it, but then the more you ponder its meaning, the more sense it makes. If we don't like ourselves first, it's pretty hard to really like anyone else— relative or not. And the only way I can really like myself is to continuously look at the positive aspects of my life. I hope you like yourself best!

MAKING EXCUSES

"I never knew a person who was good at making excuses, who was good at anything else." We got those masterful words from the great American statesman, Benjamin Franklin, who couldn't have hit it more perfectly regarding people who just don't get things done. "Too busy; didn't know about it; no time; no money; can't do it!" Those are just a few on the long list of excuses conjured up by people who often don't want to admit they don't have the courage, strengths or skills to do it. You don't need any excuses for trying. Give it a try!

BEING HONORED

President Calvin Coolidge, in one of his after dinner speeches, once told his audience, "No person was ever honored for what he received. Honor has been the reward for what he gave." Even though many people give of their time and talents, they are often never publicly honored. But to them it doesn't matter, because the reward is in the giving, and the positive feelings they receive when they know they have helped another move forward in life. Don't ever stop your giving. It is perhaps the greatest honor you can receive in life.

> **MOTIVATIONAL MINUTE #131**

A FEW BLISTERS

Abigail Van Buren has enriched many lives in this world with her uncanny, often humorous and always thoughtful answers to her readers' questions. Regarding personal motivation and working toward our goals, perhaps her best line was, "If you want a place in the sun, you have to put up with a few blisters." Blisters are the reward for a job well done, for having goals and going after them and for doing some things that some others probably thought you couldn't do. Blisters are rewarding to see, because we know we have completed something difficult.

> **MOTIVATIONAL MINUTE #132**

IT WAS ALL FUN

More than a thousand different inventions, hundreds of experiments that didn't work, failure after failure, working in bad light in a poorly heated shop. Sound like fun? Not really, but that's what Thomas Edison did for an entire lifetime. And when it was nearly over for him, he said, "I never did a day's work in my life—it was all fun!" No wonder he is considered one of our greatest success stories in America! To Edison, failure was only a challenge, and his perception was that it was all fun! Maybe what we're doing in life is fun also. Think about it!

MOTIVATIONAL MINUTE #133

IT COMES TO YOU

During the gift-giving season, many people often focus on the material goods they give or receive. But for others, the focus is on helping those who don't have what they have. Regardless of what your giving consists of, Napoleon Hill, the famous author, probably summed it up best when he told us, "If you try to bring happiness to someone else, then it comes to you." The happiness is truly in the giving, and the responses from those who receive—with their gratitude, love and appreciation. Remember, if you give it, it will always come back to you somehow!

MOTIVATIONAL MINUTE #134

ACCENTUATE THE POSITIVE

A number of years ago, Bing Crosby recorded one of his all-time greatest hits, "Accentuate the Positive (Eliminate the Negative)." Why is it that so many folks have this great need to continually focus on the negative? Such a large percentage of our lives is related to positive qualities—our personal strengths, our friends, our abilities to learn and our potential to succeed. Still, so many people continue to maintain this need to find something wrong with everything. Take some time and show yourself you can "accentuate the positive."

UP THE LADDER

Are you continuing to make improvements in your life and move in a forward direction? Andrew Carnegie, the successful industrialist of the early 20th century, once said, "You can't push anyone up a ladder unless he's willing to climb a little." By looking forward and not being willing to sit still on this rung of life you're on right now, the world knows that you are willing to climb a little. Find some friends today who might need a little push and help show them how they can make that climb much easier with a willing effort of their own.

THE VOICE WITHIN

That great leader of India, Mahatma Gandhi, believed and said many times that "the only tyrant I accept is the still voice within." One might interpret Gandhi's statement as the challenge to continually keep listening to the voice within us. It will tell us the information that no one else knows that can help us move toward personal excellence and success. The internal voice of history, of experience, of knowledge and of people is our real guide to making all our lives more productive. What is your inner voice saying today?

MOTIVATIONAL MINUTE #137

REAL LEARNING

Did you realize that learning is happening to you every minute whether or not you notice? One hundred percent of your waking day you are in the data collection business. All of that information flow goes into the brain and adds up to your total sum of learning. Today might be a good time to begin observing more closely all the things you are taking into the brain. By paying closer attention to new learning and relearning, you get much better at the difficult kind—unlearning—the kind that really moves us forward.

CHANGING THE WORLD

Margaret Mead, the wonderful sociologist, writer and speaker, once said, "Never doubt that a small group of dedicated citizens can change the world. Indeed, it's the only thing that ever has." Every change has been generated from one person's idea, shared with a small group and then completed by a group effort. Are you afraid to share your ideas with others around you? You may have the world's next great idea, so share that new idea with someone today. It may change the world for the better.

THINK FOR YOURSELF

One of the world's great thinkers, Pablo Picasso, reminds us that "Computers are useless. They can only give you answers." I'm not sure they are totally useless, since sometimes we need only answers. But we have to create the questions and to do that requires using our best computer—the brain—to think up the questions. We do have one major advantage over the computer and that is thinking for ourselves—the process of helping us reach our highest level of personal excellence. Maximize your thinking today!

MOTIVATIONAL MINUTE #140

BEING SATISFIED

The ever-popular character Popeye always says, "I am what I am." Have you asked yourself the question lately, "Who are you?" You must ask that question in order to get to the point of being able to know who you really are. And if you don't like who you are, you don't have to be satisfied. You have all the capabilities to change who you are. The first step is accepting who you are, and then moving toward who you would really like to be, asking yourself, "What do I want to do with who I am?"

MOTIVATIONAL MINUTE #141

YES, AND...?

A very creative primary teacher taught her students that the best way to lead a successful life is to use the little two-word question "Yes, and...?" "Yes, and...?" always sets you up for additional information, for more conversation and for expanded creativity. "Yes, but..." closes off any hope of change because of the put-down quality. When someone shares a new idea with you today, simply answer "Yes, and...?" You might be pleasantly surprised at how much extra you pick up, as well as the respect of the one you asked.

DOERS DO!

Before my friend Judd Holtzendorff passed away a few years ago, he shared his favorite saying with me—"Doers do!" There are so many people who talk such a good game but when it comes to the doing, they are nowhere to be found. The successful people are simply those who have done the tasks necessary to succeed. How much have you done? More importantly, what have you done lately? Take a few minutes today and think about what you have accomplished because you decided to be a "doer" instead of just a talker.

PARACHUTE BRAIN

At one of my workshops I found a little piece of paper laying on my notes after I completed the session. On the paper was written, "The mind is like a parachute—it doesn't work unless it's open." Someone had left me a reminder quote that supported my program of being open to new ideas and new directions. By maintaining an open mind you have so much more possibility of learning and growing. Just like the parachutist, if the chute doesn't open, it's over. When the parachute is open you can see for a long way.

NO FACTS

In the late 19th century, Friedrich Nietzsche was heard to say, "There are no facts, only interpretations." In other words, every fact I know is merely my interpretation of the words or the situations I observed. Everyone sees the world through different eyes, takes in data, and interprets it in a special way, then stores it in the brain. That's why communication takes skill, and willingness to listen and ask the right questions. Your facts and mine may or may not be the same. Check your facts today!

WORD OF ENCOURAGEMENT

Recently I ran across these words that some-one had shared with me: "A word of encour-agement during a failure is worth much more than a whole batch of praise after a success." You already know how good it feels when you get complimented on your successes. But it's the pat on the back, the hug or the special word from someone after you fail that really makes the positive difference. Having support from friends and others when it *didn't* work is what really helps you to try again. Find some-one who needs some help today, and share that word of encouragement.

MOTIVATIONAL MINUTE #146

MOST IMPORTANT THING

Before her death at the young age of 92, the great actress Helen Hayes made this remark about living: "The most important thing is that nothing is more important than anything else. So, I go through life having nothing but important things to do." It seems that if we all carried Miss Hayes' perception of life, we wouldn't have so many put-downs or negative judgments of others. If we would consider everything we do and say as equally important, just think how rich we could all consider ourselves to be.

MAKE A LIFE

One of my most favorite quotations is this one: "Don't be so concerned about making a living that you don't take the time to make a life." So much emphasis in our lives is put on making money, having material goods and keeping up with the neighbors. So, if being rich is what you really desire, then perhaps it's time to take stock of your inventory of *life*—your list of friends, your strengths and your potential—just to name a few *riches*. Taking the time to make a life requires that each of us first takes the time to see how rich we already are.

About the author

Don Essig is a leader with the gift for helping people discover their strengths while renewing their positive attitudes. After 30 years of being an elementary school teacher and principal, as well as a high school principal, Don left his position to go out and share his uncanny insights into human nature and motivation.

Don earned his Ph.D. in Organization Development from the University of Oregon and has been well-known in Eugene since 1967 as the "Voice of the Ducks," the public address announcer for U of O football and basketball. He is also the author of the popular book, *Personal Excellence for Key People*.

As an advocate for humane organizations, Don encourages participative leadership, enjoyable work settings and individual pursuit of excellence.

POWERFUL INSIGHTS TO IMPROVE
YOUR CAREER, YOUR BUSINESS, YOUR LIFE.

Successories, Inc. 1-800-535-2773